A King's Sanctuary

HILARY WELLINGTON

Design, typesetting and publishing by UK Book Publishing

www.ukbookpublishing.com

ISBN: 978-1-915338-21-1

For Jim and Catherine

A creative narrative based on documented historical events in and around White Ladies Manor and Boscobel House in Shropshire, England during the future King Charles II's sojourn there after the Battle of Worcester in September 1651. Seven chapters are written from the perspective of Dame Sarah Kinver, an imagined member of the household at White Ladies and three chapters are from the imagined perspective of Charles himself.

While references to the healing properties of herbs have been carefully researched, readers are strongly advised to seek the guidance of a registered medical herbalist before trying these remedies. Dosages, contra-indications and a patient's specific symptoms and requirements should always be considered with a qualified practitioner on an individual basis.

Contents

CONTENTS

Author's Preface

This little book was conceived at Boscobel House when I visited in October 2021. As I entered, a guide was telling the story of how the future King Charles II, aged just 21, arrived exhausted, soaking wet and very footsore in the early hours of Saturday 6th September 1651. He was running for his life after losing the Battle of Worcester to the Parliamentarians. They were hunting for him and would execute him if they found him.

Charles had already been helped at White Ladies Manor nearby. From there he tried to escape to Wales but had to abandon this attempt. He was guided to Boscobel by Richard Penderel, one of five remarkably brave and resourceful brothers who supported him in those first days of his time as a fugitive.

Before I visited Boscobel House, I had only known about it as the place where Charles hid in an oak tree from Cromwell's soldiers. I was quickly drawn into the rich humanity of the story and began imagining vividly how I would have cared for Charles if I had been a member of the household while he was there.

I had never viewed Charles very sympathetically before. But reading about his childhood and early adulthood has given me a very different perspective. As a child he followed his father from one battlefield to another and was sent away aged 14 to command his own troops. He was separated from his mother who had gone to France to raise funds for the Royalist cause in the Civil War. His father was imprisoned and executed. Charles endured several years of exile and impoverishment in The Hague and Scotland where he was also subjected to religious persecution, before marching south to Worcester. Then he lived on the run for six weeks, in fear for his life until he could escape back into exile in France. I now think that he was probably living with complex trauma. So, his later addictions to pleasure, food and sex might have been psychological reactions to those traumatic experiences.

Following my visit to Boscobel House, I barely slept for a fortnight. I read everything I could find about Charles' escape from Worcester and began writing the story you have here; weaving historical facts, events and people into the account of an imagined woman, Sarah, who is dedicated to serving her community with her specialist knowledge of herbal healing.

The history of medicine is often portrayed as a battle of the sexes, between male-dominated scientific knowledge, and female healing based on intuition and herbal wisdom. While there is some truth in that, the reality is not so clearly distinguished.

Before the advent of chemical pharmacology, plant-based cures were all that were available. In the 17th century all housewives would be expected to have at least a basic knowledge of these remedies and how to make them, but some women developed deeper and wider expertise. Understanding of which remedies worked for which conditions was empirical – a form of evidence-based practice, which is considered scientific today. Apothecaries might practise in larger towns and cities, but sick or injured rural people would be reliant on herbalists and wise women.

Herbalism is rooted in both monasticism and witchcraft. In mediaeval times, monasteries and convents provided early forms of hospices, caring for sick and dying people, and making remedies from herbs grown in their physic gardens. But religious communities were dissolved under King Henry VIII between 1536 and 1541 and were then heavily suppressed until the 19th century.

Women like Sarah continued the theory and practice of using herbs for healing, as a Christian vocation or for social justice (or both). In addition to herbalism, healers were often skilled in bone-setting, midwifery and laying out of deceased bodies. Midwifery licenses, which covered the broader remit of healing services, were issued by bishops but under Puritan rule from around 1646 to 1660 there were effectively no bishops. Some herbal healers worked collaboratively with male doctors. But healers were also in danger of being accused of witchcraft.

Much herbal knowledge was passed generation to generation through oral tradition and practice. Male expertise in herbal medicine was also key in disseminating knowledge. John Gerard's Herbal was published in 1597 and perhaps the more famous Nicholas

Culpeper was practising herbal medicine in the first half of the 17th century, although his books The English Physician and Complete Herbal were not published until 1652 and 1653 respectively.

Witches have also always used herbs for remedies and spells, but many women who were accused of, punished or executed for being witches, were using herbal wisdom as medical practice. Wise women and healers often lived on the edges of villages, both shunned and suspected of witchcraft while also being called upon by their community in need of a healer's services.

When medicine was developing as a profession in the early modern period, women were not admitted to British universities, and male practitioners formed associations to undermine and oppress feminine wisdom and expertise, although Culpeper also experienced ostracism as a herbalist rather than a doctor. Herbal medicine was dismissed by some doctors and physicians as folklore; and with no bishops to issue licenses, midwives and herbalists became vulnerable to slurs about being unlicensed practitioners.

The late 16th century and first half of the 17th century saw the peak of persecution of women believed to be witches. Often these were women of independent minds with strong intellects and their own financial means, considered to be a threat to the patriarchy. Secrecy and suspicion fuelled by the spiritual and political ferment of puritanism and republicanism in the 1640s and 1650s only added to rumours about healers being witches.

In the first half of the 17th century, medical knowledge (as distinguished from surgery) was largely theoretical rather than practical; and was still based on an understanding of health and disease governed by the Four Humours of blood (sanguine), yellow bile (choler), black bile and phlegm.

Medical interventions included some use of herbs alongside bloodletting and administering tinctures made from poisonous metals, ground up minerals, human bones and animal parts. When King Charles II was taken ill after an evening of feasting in February 1685, his doctors subjected him to all of the above interventions as well as applying hot irons to his head and feet to stimulate his nervous system. While well intentioned and in keeping with the practices of the period, these treatments almost certainly hastened his death, and definitely made his last few days very torturous. Antonia Fraser (2002) and Charles Spencer (2017) include accounts of Charles' end of life care in their books.

Modern medicine and pharmacology owe much to ancient herbal wisdom. Aspirin contains salicylic acid which is derived from willow. Thyme and rosemary are known to be strong antiseptics; and elderberries are now scientifically proven to have powerful anti-viral properties.

The story of bio-chemical medicine and herbal medicine is therefore more of a dichotomy than a polarity: two parts of the same whole, often in tension, sometimes more harmonious.

Charles was assisted in his escape by many courageous men and women. They all risked their own lives to protect him. In re-telling this historical account I wanted to write from a woman's perspective, using knowledge, wisdom and skills which Sarah and the other women would have used for his wellbeing.

I have also chosen to include Dorothy Giffard as the proprietor of White Ladies Manor so that she and Sarah are living, along with Mrs Andrews and Alice as a small, independent community of women. English Heritage, which owns White Ladies, places Dorothy in that position at the time of Charles' visit, although other sources name different people, male and female, as the owners or tenants.

Hilary Wellington, *January 2022*

Historical Characters

Mrs Andrews: Cook and Housekeeper at White Ladies Manor. It is documented that a Mrs Andrews worked as a cook/housekeeper at White Ladies, although some versions of events place her there as John or Charles Giffard's housekeeper

Major William Carlis: A Cavalier officer who fought at the Battle of Worcester, defending His Majesty's escape. He took refuge at Boscobel House over the same weekend as Charles

Cavaliers: Soldiers loyal to the Crown and fighting for the King in the Civil War

Oliver Cromwell: Head of the Republican Commonwealth which lasted from 1649 to 1660 and Lord Protector of England (1653-1658), leader of the New Model Army also known as the Roundheads and Parliamentarian troops. He was a strict Protestant Puritan opposed to Roman Catholicism and celebration of religious ritual and social festivals

Cromwell's soldiers of the New Model Army: Soldiers fighting against Charles's army at the Battle of Worcester and searching for him in the house raid at White Ladies and in the woods at Boscobel House

Gentlemen of the Bedchamber: Lords and other aristocratic men who attended to the King by helping him dress, waiting on him at table and providing companionship

Charles Giffard: Cousin or nephew of Dorothy Giffard, who fought for the King at Worcester and directed him to White Ladies on the night of his escape from the city

Mistress Dorothy Giffard: Widowed owner of White Ladies Manor (although some sources have John or Charles Giffard living there, or Mistress Frances Cotton who was said to be away from the house when Charles arrived).

Father John Huddleston: Benedictine monk living at Moseley Hall under the protection of Mr Whitgreave. He cared for Charles in his time at Moseley Hall; and in his old age, he received King Charles II into the Roman Catholic Church on his death bed

Her Majesty Queen Henrietta Maria: Mother of King Charles II, widow of King Charles I and aunt of King Louis XIV of France

His Majesty King Charles I: Charles' father, who was executed on 30th January 1649 by Parliamentarians

His Majesty Charles Stuart: At the time of his sanctuary at White Ladies and Boscobel House, he was King of Scotland but not of England, Wales and Ireland. He travelled on from Boscobel under assumed names of William Jones and William Jackson on his journey escaping England after the Battle of Worcester

His Majesty King Louis XIV of France: 'The Sun King' who was a maternal cousin to Charles II.

His Royal Highness Prince James, Duke of York: Younger brother to Charles II, and the future King James II

Colonel Lane: Owner of Bentley Hall from where Charles escaped to Bristol disguised as a servant

Mistress Jane Lane: Sister of Colonel Lane, who had permission from the authorities to travel to be with her pregnant friend in Bristol and rode pillion with Charles disguised as her manservant

The Miller at Evelith: Challenged Charles and Richard Penderel and later was discovered to be a Royalist who was on guard because he was sheltering Cavalier soldiers

George Penderel: Caretaker and woodsman at White Ladies Manor

Humphrey Penderel: Miller at White Ladies Mill, and owner of the horse which Charles rode to Moseley Hall

Mistress Joan Penderel: Wife of William Penderel, both tenants of Boscobel House

John Penderel: Woodsman at White Ladies Manor, and in some historical accounts he fought for the King at the Battle of Worcester and was in the party which escorted Charles safely away from Worcester

Mistress Penderel: Wife of Richard Penderel

Richard Penderel: Tenant farmer at Hobbal Grange near Tong in Shropshire. He had experience of hiding and disguising Roman Catholic priests from the Puritan authorities

William Penderel: Tenant of Boscobel House

Mr Thomas Whitgreave: Owner of Moseley Hall where Charles was taken after his stay at Boscobel House

Lord Henry Wilmot: Cavalier soldier and confidant of King Charles who acted as a broker arranging accommodation for Charles as he journeyed southwest to Lyme Regis and then eastwards along the south coast to Shoreham in Sussex where they both safely boarded a coal boat to France after six weeks on the run

Francis Wolfe: Owner or tenant of Upper House in Madeley, a village on the east bank of the River Severn

Mistress Wolfe: Wife of Francis Wolfe, credited in some historical accounts with darkening Charles' skin with walnut juice

Mistress Eleanor (Nell) Yates: Sister to the Penderel brothers, married to Francis. She took food to Charles on his first day in hiding

Francis Yates: Brother-in-law to the Penderels, who helped to keep Charles safe in the woods at White Ladies and at Boscobel

Fictional Characters

Alice: A very shy young girl of about 13 years old, in service as a housemaid at White Ladies Manor

Dame Sarah Kinver: A devout Catholic gentlewoman, helper and companion to Mistress Dorothy Giffard, and herbalist

White Ladies Manor, Thursday Morning 4th September 1651: Sarah

The commotion started just before dawn. A sound which I later realised to be muffled hooves mingled with my dream, taking me back into my father's orchard, riding my beloved Welsh pony, Demoiselle.

But then I was jolted awake by barking dogs and hammering on the door. Fearing it would be Parliamentarian soldiers demanding entry to search for recusant priests, I leapt out of bed and rushed to the top of the stairs. There I met my cousin Dorothy Giffard, dowager mistress of the house, under whose protection I live as her companion and helper. She was deathly pale and shaking. "A search party?" I asked. As a Roman Catholic household living under Puritan rule, we had thought there might be a raid on our house soon after the fighting at Worcester ended, some thirty miles away.

"No," Dorothy replied, lowering her voice to a whisper. "His Majesty is come with John Penderel and my nephew Charles from battle at Worcester. He arrived with a retinue of Lords and Gentlemen of the Bedchamber, but they have quickly departed to draw attention away from our house. The battle is lost because the Scots would not fight for His Majesty, and he is now a fugitive." As staunch Royalists we call Prince Charles by this title even though Cromwell's iron grip now kept him from taking his place as King in England. Dorothy grasped my wrist urgently, "Sarah, go to him and tend to him. He's in the parlour. He's bone weary and chilled through. Have little Alice stoke the fire and ask Mrs Andrews to prepare a posset for him. George Penderel has gone to Hobbal Grange to fetch his brother, Richard. They will come with workmen's clothes to disguise His Majesty."

I did as I was bidden pausing only to gather a blanket and my basket which I filled with dried lavender, rosemary, yarrow, and a new concoction called Epsom Salts from the cupboard which serves as my stillroom. Healing is my sacred calling. If I had been born before the Dissolution of the Monasteries, I would almost certainly have served as Infirmarian at a convent like White Ladies, among the ruins of which my cousin's manor house now stands.

There was a horse in the hall, a great grey stallion. He was still covered in dried sweat from the heat of battle, and his legs were slathered in mud. His eyes were wild and white with alarm, and he tossed his mane and snorted hard as I passed by. With my arms full, I could do nothing to reassure him except to speak gently and blow softly into his flaring nostrils, which has a calming effect on horses. Through the window I could see John coming to the house with a pail of water from the well and a net full of hay for the charger. He was being well cared for and my duty was to his master in the parlour.

His Majesty was huddled, shivering with cold, fear or shock, by the fire while our sweet housemaid Alice stacked it with good, dry logs from our woods. He was pumping the bellows to ignite more flame and trying to engage Alice in quiet conversation, but although she gazed at him with her big brown eyes and smiled, she was too much in awe of him to speak to him. I thanked her with a smile and asked her to bring a basin of hot water and a muslin cloth for me. Then I made a deep curtsey and kissed His Majesty's icy hand in a gesture of fealty. "Your Majesty, a thousand welcomes. Rest now, and warm yourself. We are all at your service and will do everything in our power to keep you safe. I am Sarah, cousin and helpmeet to Mistress Dorothy," I explained. He returned my kiss, his lips cold on my hand. "Dame Sarah, I thank you for your welcome and am delighted to make your acquaintance." I held out the blanket and he yielded to being swaddled in it for more warmth, leaning into my arms, much in need of comfort after the horrors of battle.

Just then, Alice came back into the parlour with a posset and a dish of oats, cream, honey and nutmeg, closely followed by Mrs Andrews with the water. His Majesty's hands were too numb to hold the dish of porridge, so he handed it to me and I fed him. Some colour began to come into his cheeks and his shaking lessened. "Your Majesty, are you wounded from battle?" I enquired. "No," he replied, "but my bones ache from riding all

night, and as you have felt and seen, I am very chilled."
"Then, Sire, may I bathe your feet?" I asked. "If the feet
are comforted, the body is also." He stretched out his
long legs to allow me to remove his stockings and dipped
his bare feet into the water, to which I had added the salts
to soothe his bones and the herbs to drive out infection
and calm his mind. I gently washed his feet, and felt
his muscles relax as he sighed with relief and pleasure.
Presently, George the caretaker of White Ladies and his
brother Richard Penderel entered the parlour with an
armful of countrymen's clothing. Richard is a farmer
who has become very skilled at hiding the identities
of Catholic priests and Cavaliers who frequently seek
sanctuary at houses like White Ladies and Boscobel
House on the Giffard family's estate. They greeted His
Majesty and began to explain their plan for his disguise
as a woodsman as I dried his feet.

Meanwhile the brothers were observing His Majesty's
long, dark locks. "Sire," began Richard, apologetically,
"we regret that unless we cut your hair, any disguise
we can provide will not be sufficient to protect you."
His Majesty's expression became very downcast, but
he nodded. "It grieves me sorely, but I know that you
are right. Better to lose my hair than my life." I could
not help myself from exclaiming, "Oh, my poor lamb!"
His Majesty looked directly at me and asked, "Then
Dame Sarah, will you be my shearer?" My hand flew
to my mouth. It horrified me to think of cutting off his
beautiful long curls, but I was so moved that he would
trust me. I bowed my head and said, "Sire, it saddens
me as much as you, but I will reverently do this in your

service to save your sweet life, and I thank you deeply for trusting me with this task." Richard proffered a pair of sheep shears, but I declined, knowing that I would trust myself better with my needlework scissors than rough shears made to be handled by a man's large hands.

There was no time to waste. Excusing myself, I fled upstairs, unable to stem the tears coursing down my cheeks. I collected my scissors, took up my own hairbrush and comb, and snatched up my night shawl to cover His Majesty's shirt while I cut his hair. There was just time to make my daily prayer as I went back downstairs, "Strengthen my hands in thy holy service, O Lord." Never had it been more heartfelt.

Back in the parlour, the men were discussing a name and character under which His Majesty was to travel on from our house. They agreed on William Jones, a Worcestershire woodsman. Richard was holding up a jacket against His Majesty to test for size. I wondered how any clothing he had would fit His Majesty who is much the tallest man I have ever seen, head and shoulders above Richard and George.

"Gentlemen," I asked, "pray, a little privacy for His Majesty while I cut his hair?" The Penderel brothers obliged, and I was again alone with this young man, at once so powerful and so vulnerable. "Your Majesty, I beg forgiveness for this grievous injury I must do you," I murmured, as I settled him into a more upright chair and wrapped him in my shawl. "Sweet Mistress Sarah, I know you would never wittingly cause me harm. This gives us both sorrow, but I know you will do it tenderly, and that you do it out of love for me." Such words! That the rightful king of England should call me "sweet" and say that he knew my actions came from love for him.

I had to work quickly. At any moment, Parliamentarian soldiers could be at the door; but I so wanted this to feel nurturing and unhurried for him. His hair was very tangled after battle and his long, urgent night-time ride. I brushed it gently before taking up my scissors and starting to snip off those glorious black curls, just above his shoulders at first, although more would have to come off to make him less recognisable. And as so often happens when hair is cut short, a flood of emotion overtook him. Indeed, we wept together for the sacrifice of his hair, for his executed father and the people forced to live and die under Cromwell's cruel regime; he for the men and horses he had lost in the dreadful Battle of Worcester, and I with fear for his safety in the days to come. Quite spontaneously we reached out for each other, and I cradled him in my arms. For all his royal status he was but a lad of twenty-one, who had already lived through unimaginable heartbreak and now found himself hunted like a wild animal by people intent on dealing him the same death they had inflicted on his blessed father. He needed a mother's love and comfort, but Queen Henrietta Maria was far away in Paris. Through my tears I softly sang him a lullaby and gently rocked him, which seemed to soothe him.

Once we were composed again, I continued snipping his hair, more precisely this time, studying how his curls lay and cutting along the length I'd left so that his hair fell naturally to his collar and around his ears, framing his face with soft waves. I surprised myself by starting to feel happy with the result. His Majesty seemed to intuit my change of mood and he asked if I could show him his new haircut in a looking glass. He gasped with shock at first at such a drastic change but then he smiled and considered his image carefully from different angles, ruffling his newly shorn locks before declaring himself very pleased. He took my hand in his and kissed it again, warmly, lingeringly this time, and said, "Thank you, sweet Sarah. You have done me a most excellent favour and I will never forget this great kindness." I curtsied again and told him that it was a great privilege for me to serve him in this way.

It was now my turn to give His Majesty some privacy while Richard and George dressed him. They exclaimed at his transformation as I hastily swept up the cut hair. I would have dearly loved to save at least one lock as a keepsake but knew that if, or when, the house were raided, any showing that the King had been here and of what had been done to disguise him would put him and our household in imminent mortal danger. So, ruefully I carried the clippings through to the kitchen to burn them on the fire. I couldn't bear to let His Majesty see his hair being thrown like dross onto the fire in the parlour. Mrs Andrews gaped in amazement, and it was all too much for Alice, who burst into tears. I knelt down beside her to reassure her that I had cut William's - as we now must call him – hair with great care and that he truly liked his new haircut. She ran to her box bed by the kitchen fire and pulled a knitted woollen cap from the little cupboard she had there. I knew she had made it for her father but she whispered, "I should like William to have it because he will need something to keep his head warm now." I said she should come with me when William was dressed in his new clothes and present it to him herself, and that I would help her to make a new one to give to her father.

Dorothy joined us in the kitchen, having been keeping watch from the attic for Parliamentarian soldiers. Her round cheeks had recovered some ruddiness, and she bustled about the kitchen making sure there was food enough for our unexpected guest to eat later in the day. Suddenly we heard a burst of male laughter from the parlour, and the three men came out, slapping each other on the back and joking.

Despite my concerns about finding clothes to fit, His Majesty was now dressed in a shirt of coarse, unbleached linen, workmen's rough breeches and a leather doublet. I recognised the doublet as Richard's own and judging from the length of the breeches I guessed those must belong to William Penderel, the tenant of Boscobel House who is considered a very tall man hereabouts. Our William had a felted grey hat pulled low on his forehead, and workers' shoes which looked uncomfortable to him in place of his beautiful leather riding boots. On seeing us he doffed his hat with a flourish, made a bow and greeted us in a very convincing Worcestershire accent, telling us his new name and that he was looking for woodsman's work.

Alice was entranced and crept forward to give him the woollen cap which I explained to His Majesty she wanted him to have because she was so concerned for him feeling the cold now his hair was cut short. He crouched down and whispered to her, "Sweet maid, how kind you are to think of me. I shall treasure your gift and think on you whenever I wear it." Then he kissed her gently on the cheek, which made her blush and run giggling back to the larder where she was engaged in churning butter. Cousin Dorothy spoke now: "Well met, William Jones. I have work for a woodsman in my coppice. Richard will take you there now to begin, and at noon I shall send out a lunch to sustain you in your work." Richard beamed. "The perfect decoy while we plot your escape, Your Majesty – I mean, William. Who would suspect two workers in a copse, pruning dead wood? How clever you are, Mistress Dorothy." He handed our William a billhook and summoned him to work.

White Ladies Manor, Thursday Afternoon 4th September 1651: Sarah

O nce Richard and our William had left the house, those of us remaining exchanged long looks of wonderment at what had just occurred. Then George made the sign of the cross and we all knelt to pray for God's safe keeping of his brother and our King.

We then went about our usual morning's work, but more watchfully and warily than ever. John had been caring for His Majesty's charger while his brothers and I had disguised him. The horse was calmer now as John finished grooming him. He explained to me that Lord Henry Wilmot, a confidant of His Majesty had escaped towards Moseley Hall. John would ride His Majesty's horse to be stabled there once he and the horse had rested a little more, and Dorothy's nephew Charles Giffard would accompany John with a spare horse for him to ride home. It was Charles, said John, who had directed His Majesty to White Ladies in the night, having been in his army with John at Worcester.

I sat for a while in my chamber with some household linens which were needful of mending, although in truth my head and heart were so full that I was too restive to give myself to the task. Every few stitches I would find myself looking out of the window, scanning the horizon and nearby lanes and fields for signs of approaching troops. Then my mind would turn to how astonishing and moving it was that our King should suffer me to crop his royal locks. I wept a little more for the loss of his precious hair, quietly, so as not to disturb the rest of the household. Presently I decided that some fresh air was required, so I ventured out into my herb garden to gather hyssop and thyme to make tinctures to counter pain and infections, chamomile and lemon balm to make tisanes to soothe unquiet minds and winter colds.

At noon, George and I set off to walk to Spring Coppice with a basket of broth, some biscuit and small beer for Richard and our William's midday meal. We found His Majesty sitting on a blanket which Richard had borrowed from his brother-in-law Francis Yates, who was keeping guard with him. It was raining and all three men looked dejected and cold, so they were very glad of the broth to warm them, along with a set mixture of eggs, milk and cheese which Francis' good wife Nell had brought for them. His Majesty asked me to be sure to tell Alice how grateful he was already for the comfort of his new cap which he had on underneath his grey hat, and he showed me his hands which had already roughened a little under Richard's tutelage of cutting coppice poles.

They had all periodically done some manual work to keep out some of the cold and damp, and Richard had gathered a goodly bundle of dead wood for George to carry back to the house for kindling. Francis had found a wilding apple tree in the lane he was guarding and had a pile of apples ready for Nell and me to fill our baskets. The chief task of the morning, however, had been for Richard and our William to draw up a plan of escape. Richard took George to one side, and told him, as George reported to me afterwards, that he had persuaded His Majesty to give up his quest to make for London, and they had agreed instead to walk westwards at nightfall to the Penderels' friend Francis Wolfe's house, hoping to go on into Wales to one of the ports and sail from there to France.

We wished them "Godspeed," and set off to return to White Ladies, the apples atop my basket which held the remains of the men's meal. I was much troubled about our William and Richard walking in the chill of the night while they were already damp. His Majesty had endured harrowing days of battle and had not rested overnight. With these worries on my mind, I spied some goodly elderberries in the hedgerow and stopped to pick them for making syrup, which is a most excellent tonic against feverish chills.

George had gone on a little way in front of me when I heard a loud shout of "Halt!" and looking ahead I saw him surrounded by four Parliamentarian soldiers on horseback. My stomach churned but I tried to calm myself in the knowledge that His Majesty was very well disguised and was in very safe company.

The officer in charge, a lean, hard-faced captain of the New Model Army, was questioning George, when another soldier saw me and briskly rode his sturdy bay horse towards me. He was very young, a sallow faced lad of no more than eighteen years, I would guess. But he was keen to impress his captain. "Woman, put down your basket and come hither. What is your business here?" he ordered me. I complied and answered as steadily as I could, although my heart was pounding in my chest. "Good day, sir. I have been harvesting apples and am returning home to White Ladies," I explained, hoping to Heaven that he would not inspect the basket and find the crockery. "And what else are you gathering?" he probed. "I have elderberries from this hedgerow tree to make cough syrup," I told him. His hazel eyes narrowed to a piercing stare. "Are you a witch, Mistress, that you make such potions?" he interrogated. "Nay sir," I replied, "elderberry syrup is a commonplace country remedy for coughs and feverish chills. I make it every autumn for my household." From his ignorance of such matters, I deemed he must be city-bred.

I could hear George explaining his position at White Ladies and denying that the King had been seen hereabouts. The captain told him menacingly that anyone found harbouring the king would be punished by certain death. The young soldier who had questioned me now pushed me forward roughly towards his captain, causing me to stumble against my basket and spill some of the elderberries. Mercifully the apples must have been so tightly packed in that there was no rattle from the crockery. "Sir!" he called to his commander, "this woman has been harvesting hedgerow berries to make concoctions that sound like witches' brews." The officer regarded me contemptuously and sneered. "Witches' brews, eh? Well, maybe this old maid can conjure a spell for us to capture the fugitive. There's a £1000 bounty on the traitor Charles Stuart's head. 'T would make a very fine dowry for the likes of her." The rest of the soldiers laughed derisively. "Sir, I am neither a witch nor an old maid, but a country gentlewoman serving God in the care for my household. I am simply gathering elderberries to make medicaments," I countered. The officer's face softened for a moment. "Elderberry syrup, eh? My grandmother used to make that for me when I was a boy." Then his features grew stern again and he ordered his men to escort George and me back to the house under armed guard. I was forced to leave my basket behind.

When we arrived, the house was in uproar. Four more soldiers had Dorothy, John Penderel who mercifully had arrived back from Moseley Hall, Mrs Andrews and little Alice corralled in the hall. One of the soldiers was interrogating them and Alice was sobbing, her head buried in Mrs Andrews' apron so only her mobcap was visible.

Another soldier shouted at Alice to be quiet which only made her cry more. As we were bundled into the hall the captain who had questioned George and me took charge. He sent three soldiers to search the kitchen and parlour and another three to search upstairs. He kept the young soldier who had stopped me with him to block our exit. "Are there any more in your household?" the officer barked at Dorothy. "Speak true, or else it will go very badly for you all." "Nay sir," replied Dorothy. "We are a small household and are all hereby accounted for." "And what of any you might be harbouring?" the officer probed. "I remind you, the punishment for concealing the traitor we seek is death without mercy." "Sir, there is none here except those you see before you, and neither has there been since my dear husband died this twelve-month past." Dorothy protested.

From where we stood, we could see the soldiers dragging books from the shelves in the parlour and knocking paintings off the walls. Then they began to pull out the panelling, intent on finding a hiding place and a fugitive king. Having found nothing untoward, they repaired to the kitchen, and we could hear them pulling crockery from the cupboards. Upstairs, their heavy boots trampled through the rooms testing floorboards for weak spots which might betray a priest hole, tearing curtains and hangings down, determined to do as much damage as they could. Then I realised they had found my stillroom. I could hear them smashing jars and bottles of the precious herbs and spices I had laid aside to comfort and heal my household in the cold months. Even though my conscience was perfectly clear of any witchcraft, I was very much afeared the officer in charge would, even so, arrest me for a witch and I felt so wretchedly sorry for Dorothy whose house they were wrecking. I could see that her bosom was heaving with barely suppressed outrage at the destruction, but she knew that to protest would risk more than their despicable vandalism.

The soldiers had completed their malevolent work in the house and were now sent out to search the stables and outbuildings. While they were gone, the captain called me to him, pinned me to himself with his arm across my collarbone and cocked his flintlock under my chin, threatening me that if his soldiers had found anything that they suspected of being other than innocent country remedies in my stillroom he would see me hanged for a witch. I tried very hard not to tremble, but he must surely have felt how hard and fast my heart was pounding. I know of several sister herbalists who have been put through the ordeal of witchcraft trials and some who have been executed, despite only using herbs for healing.

The soldiers came back to the house from their search in the farmyard and reported finding nothing of suspicion. The captain then addressed Dorothy in his cold, sinister voice, saying, "Mistress Giffard, we know you belong to a Catholic and Royalist family and that you employ such on your estate. Be advised that we are watching your house very closely and just because we have not found him whom we seek today, that does not mean that we might not return." They made ready to go, but not before roughly shoving John and George around, thrusting their pistols menacingly into their chests and issuing further threats to all our lives if they did find we had been sheltering the king.

Once they were out of sight poor Dorothy collapsed on the flagstones in the hall, releasing all her pent-up fury and fear. Mrs Andrews and I went to comfort her. John ran to fetch a cup of small beer to give her, and we sat her up so she could drink it. "Look what they've done!" she shrieked. "Look what those villains have done to my house! They have ransacked it! How shall we ever repair this damage? I can't stay here. I cannot!" I had to confess that I had no heart to do so either. George and John surveyed the damage and declared that they could repair almost all of it, but this would take them several days at least. I could not face assessing the havoc wreaked in my stillroom.

We were all very shaken by our ordeal, and I made a large pot of camomile tea to calm our frayed nerves. Poor George and John had taken a physical battering, and we had all been threatened with death. We discussed whether we should send Alice home to her family under a pretence of illness, but the men thought this might arouse further suspicion, and Alice clung to me and said she wanted to stay. Dear Mrs Andrews hugged me and declared, "We would never let them take you for a witch, Dame Sarah, my duckie. Ooh, when that captain had his pistol under your chin, I wanted to floor him with my rolling pin. Everyone knows you're a holy woman and no witch!" I thanked her for her kind words but reminded her that not everyone always sees a clear distinction between holy healing and witchcraft.

We decided that we must seek sanctuary ourselves from our devastated home. John and George were sent trudging out to request lodgings for Dorothy and Mrs Andrews with Giffard relatives at Black Ladies in the village of Brewood a mile or so away, while I would take Alice under my guardianship with me to Boscobel if

William Penderel and his wife Joan could accommodate us. We made ready to leave with the few belongings we could retrieve. The Giffards very kindly sent their ostler with a horse and trap to transport Dorothy and Mrs Andrews, while Alice and I loaded our possessions into paniers for Dorothy's pet donkey to carry with us as we walked the mile to Boscobel House.

To Madeley and Back:
Thursday night and Friday
5th September 1651: Charles

Richard and I spent a long, wet day in Spring Coppice, ostensibly cutting wood, but in fact working out a plan for my escape. I had intended to go to London to rally my troops and supporters, but Richard persuaded me that this was too dangerous. He has an astute mind, and suggested instead that he should escort me under cover of darkness to his friend Francis Wolfe's house some nine miles west in a village called Madeley, and from there to cross the River Severn and head towards Swansea and find a ship sailing for France. I knew that Cromwell had less support in Wales and that I would be in less danger there. The prospect of walking in the shoes Richard had given me filled me with trepidation as they were already pinching and chafing my feet sorely, and I had not walked above half a mile in them. What I most wanted was to be warm and dry and to feel safe, but I knew it would be a long time before I could be, and that I must walk those nine miles and possibly many more if I were ever to be safe again.

As dusk fell, Richard showed me the way to his farmhouse, where we ate bread and cheese and drank small beer to fortify us for our journey. There was a tense atmosphere as Richard's wife made her feelings known. She was angry that Richard had spent his day and would now give up the night and next day helping me. She glowered at me from the kitchen, and I could hear her goading Richard to turn me over to the Parliamentarians. "If you don't do it, someone else will afore you get him safe to Wales, and just think of how we would be set for life with that reward. We could buy a farm and no longer have to live as tenants. We could live in comfort instead of having to scrape a living. Fact is, if you don't turn him in, I might just do it anyways," she threatened. I couldn't overhear Richard's response, as he bundled his wife out of the back door into the yard, but I could tell from his tone that he was rebuking her. After the loyalty and honour the Penderel brothers and the household at White Ladies had shown me all day, Mistress Penderel's hostility shocked me and forced me to confront the fragility of my life as a hunted man. It would be that easy for someone, anyone, to betray me to the Puritan authorities.

Once the moon was high, we set off. Richard knows the country around Hobbal Grange like the back of his hand and guided me well. As I feared though, my feet were much afflicted by the shoes which were now wet from a rainy day in the coppice. I hobbled along as well as I could and as soon as the time seemed opportune, I confronted Richard about the discussion he had had with his wife. "Can she be trusted, Richard? Is my life as good as over?" "Nay Sire," he answered, "I have put a stop to her notion by telling her that if she betrays you, she will lose me as well. Besides, we are a family faithful to the Crown. She would not carry out her threat. She is disgruntled that this work I do takes me away from the farm." I tried hard to let Richard's words settle my mind, but the exchange I had witnessed in the kitchen had been very disquieting.

We were making such progress as was possible for me along rough lanes in those shoes, when we heard laughter and saw a light ahead. Richard explained we were near Evelith Mill, and he could see the miller standing in his doorway, his white smock picked out between the moonlight and the candlelit interior. We were about to divert across a field when the miller heard our footsteps and called out, "Who goes there?" Richard answered that we were friends returning home, but the miller was suspicious and called his companions out to challenge us, with a cry of "Rogues, rogues!" There was just time enough for us to leap behind a hedge where we had to huddle until the shouting abated and the light in the mill went out. Our hiding place was muddy and rank, and our already damp and cold joints began to stiffen while we dare not move.

Once we were walking again our progress slowed. The moon had disappeared behind clouds and gave no light to show us the way in countryside which was less familiar to Richard than the first few miles had been. I fell behind him which made me much afeared that we should be separated. Richard waited patiently for me, but I could sense that he was anxious about the time the journey was taking us. Thank God that we encountered nobody else that night.

After what seemed an eternity, we came to a settlement which Richard recognised as Madeley and he led me to Upper House where his friend Francis Wolfe lives. I hid myself in a small stand of beech trees while Richard went to make our introductions. I could just make out a light in the doorway and muffled voices. From the length and tone of the discourse it seemed that Mr Wolfe was somewhat reluctant to harbour a distressed Cavalier. But then I heard footsteps coming towards me and Richard was beside me again. "Sire," he whispered, "Mr Wolfe said he would not risk his neck for anyone but the King. So, I have had to reveal your true identity to secure you safe passage into his house. But I assure you that Mr Wolfe a fervent supporter of Your Majesty. He is very anxious because his son has been taken prisoner of war at Worcester and transported to Shrewsbury."

He ushered me towards the house, where Mr Wolfe let us in but could not hide his discomfort at sheltering a fugitive whose life - and the lives of those who harboured him - hung in the balance. "Sire, I am not at all at peace with this. I will give you food and drink but must ask you after that to hide yourself in my hayloft rather than my house. If you were discovered it would be the end of my whole family, my son being taken prisoner after the Battle of Worcester. You should know also, Sire, that Parliamentarian soldiers are hard by, and have the river and crossings closely patrolled. Richard has told me of your plan to cross the Severn and on into Wales, but I must warn you that it is gravely risky." This news dismayed me greatly. I had been so glad to reach Madeley and had hoped for a welcome of the kind I had received at White Ladies. My feet were blistered and swollen, and I wanted above anything at that moment to sleep.

Presently Mr Wolfe's good wife brought us possets and biscuit and looked pityingly at Richard and me. We must indeed have been a sorry sight in our countrymen's clothes which were stained and wet from our trudge through the dark lanes and fields. As soon as we had finished the refreshment, Mr Wolfe chivvied us out of the house and into his barn. The ground floor was crowded with his cattle and held a muggy and rancid air. He showed us to a ladder which led us into the hayloft. "Rest here awhile, Your Majesty," he told me. "Richard will stay with you for now, but once he has rested and the sun is up, he and I will walk out to the river. I cannot think but it will be as closely guarded as it was yesterday."

Richard and I lay down, thankful for now at least for a dry place to rest. The hay smelled sweet, and I tried to fill my nostrils with that aroma to block out the noisome ones from the cattle shed. "Try to sleep, Sire," advised Richard. "I will keep watch until Mr Wolfe returns." My eyelids were so heavy I would gladly have fallen to slumber, but my mind was racing anxiously about what I would do now. Wales seemed impossible to reach, and I knew not whether Richard had other friends hereabouts who might harbour me. I supposed that they would be as much on their guard as Mr Wolfe; and any house known to be loyal to the King would be watched closely by Cromwell's men. I could almost feel them closing in on me.

I made myself as comfortable as I could in the hay and tried to quieten my mind, but sleep would not come. Before long, Mr Wolfe returned to ask Richard to accompany him towards the river. Richard, who, like me, had not slept since before dawn the day before, got up and followed Mr Wolfe without protest. I had not met with men like Richard and his brothers before, but I thanked God for the trusty companion he was. Mr Wolfe led his cattle out into the field which at least stopped any addition to the stench. It was very quiet in the barn without them, but this made me more vigilant than before. At every creak of the timbers, every rustle of a rat or mouse in the hay, I was on my mettle.

Even if I had been able to settle my thoughts, I would have been kept from sleep by the aching of my limbs and the pain of the blisters and cuts on my feet. Despite the breakfast, I was hungry and very thirsty. Many times during that long, lonely day I thought of Mistress Sarah and her gentle care and compassion. How I wished she were with me now to bathe and doctor my feet with her healing herbs, and comfort me in her arms as she had done yesterday.

After some hours Mr Wolfe and Richard returned with a young man whom it transpired was Mr Wolfe's son returned from imprisonment. This good news was tempered by the other news they brought. They confirmed what Mr Wolfe had told us that morning. The river would not afford us a safe way into Wales. They had roved for miles and had seen soldiers as far as the eye could see. Richard explained that our only choices were to walk south and take our chances of finding another house which would shelter us, or to return to either to White Ladies or to Boscobel House near there. Both felt very dangerous but at least we knew that we would be sure of a welcome back at our previous haven whereas to take the former choice would risk walking straight into a Parliamentarian ambush.

At dusk, Mr Wolfe took us back to Upper House where Mistress Wolfe had kindly prepared for us a dinner of cold beef, eggs and lettuce from the kitchen garden, which we ate gratefully. I could hardly contain my desperation to partake of the small beer she brought to the table, having had nothing to drink since breakfast. Mistress Wolfe knew well enough that I was a Cavalier fugitive, and on noticing the whiteness of my hands took it upon herself to swab them and my face with walnut juice which she said would make my complexion appear more weather beaten like to that of a country woodsman.

The walk back towards White Ladies is one I can scarcely remember. I was so weary and sore that all I could do was to put one painful foot in front of the other, almost mechanically. Perhaps I even walked in my sleep. Our journey must have passed without meeting other travellers, although we had to ford a river when Richard took me on a diversion to avoid going back past

Evelith Mill. The water was deeper and faster flowing than we expected, and for once it was myself who led the way, being more confident in water than Richard. The coldness of the water at least numbed the pain in my feet for a short while.

At long last Richard informed me that we were back in the vicinity of White Ladies. He supposed that it was very likely that the house would have been raided by now and decided we should make our way instead to Boscobel House which stood away from the highway, surrounded by woodland. Richard led me through fields which were so familiar to him that even on a moonless night like this he knew his way. We came to a covert of oaks, and he bade me wait for him there while he went to rouse his brother William at Boscobel. Now we had stopped walking I realised how chilled I was, and sat shuddering with cold and fatigue, barely able to keep myself awake.

I know not how long I waited there, drifting in and out of consciousness, but suddenly I was startled by a shout. The voice sounded familiar, but I could not place it at first. Then came two figures running – Richard's sturdy, dependable frame which I had followed over many miles, and another man whom I recognised as he came close as one of my stalwart officers, Major Carlis, whom I had supposed dead at the end of the Battle of Worcester. I had last seen him leading a desperate charge down New Street towards Sidbury Gate to prevent Cromwell's men from blocking my escape from the city. He knelt to me and reached for my hand to kiss it. "Sire," he panted,

"I am glad indeed to see you. The Roundheads have been spreading the news abroad that you were killed at Worcester. My poor master, your strength is all spent. Come, let us help you into the house." I was very glad to see him alive too. He and Richard, who must also have been exhausted, each took one of my arms over their shoulders, made a seat for me by linking their free arms and carried me to the house.

Arrival at Boscobel: Saturday Morning 6th September 1651: Sarah

A t about three of the clock in the middle of the night, there came such a thumping on the door that the whole household of Boscobel, like that of White Ladies two nights previously, was startled from our slumbers. Poor Major Carlis, one of His Majesty's officers who had defended him so valiantly at the Battle of Worcester, and who had arrived at Boscobel yesterday, bolted for the priest hole much afeared his life was in immediate danger from a Parliamentarian search party.

William went cautiously to the door and called stoutly, "Who goes there?" His own brother Richard's voice answered, and William flung the door wide. Richard staggered over the threshold alone and fell onto the settle. He was panting, wet through and plainly exhausted. "Richard, what news?" gasped William. Richard waited until the door was safely closed before he answered, "The border into Wales is unsafe. Cromwell's troops have it heavily guarded. We could not stay at Francis Wolfe's house and have had to walk back. His Majesty is waiting in the wood beyond our pasture, for fear the house here

is under siege. Is it safe? I will go back for him if so."
By now, Major Carlis had joined us in the hall and was
most eager to go with Richard, who warned him that
the King was in great pain and at the point of collapse.

As the two men left to retrieve His Majesty, we began
our preparations to tend to him and Richard. William
lit the fire from the previous night's embers, and Joan set
a cauldron of water to heat over the fire, before busying
herself in making possets to revive the two exhausted
wayfarers. Without recourse to my stillroom, I felt rather
helpless, but knew I must make the best of any resources
I could quickly gather from the kitchen. Joan allowed
me to take some sea salt from her pantry with which to
bathe His Majesty's sore feet, and she watched anxiously
as I cut a precious slice of new honeycomb to use as a
salve. She had some rosemary drying in a bunch hung
from a beam and gave me a large sprig of it for cleansing
His Majesty's wounds. I then ran to the linen press to
collect towels, clean nightshirts, blankets and strips of
linen to serve as bandages. I hoped it would soon grow
light enough for me to venture outside to the garden,
where I might find fresh herbs, and willow, the bark
of which provides a most effective relief to pain and
inflammation.

Presently there came another knocking on the door, and
William, who had been waiting by it, made sure it was
his brother before pulling the door wide open again.
Richard and Major Carlis carried a pitifully exhausted
man, whom I barely recognised as His Majesty, over
the threshold. He fell from their hold and collapsed on

the stone flags. He was gaunt with hunger and pain; and soaked to the skin, his wet hair plastered to his head. His complexion had taken on a strange shade of brown which made me even more anxious for his health. William and Major Carlis lifted our King again and carried him to the fireside chair in the parlour before going back to draw Richard in from the hall.

It was evident to us all with no need for speech, that we must work urgently as a household to save His Majesty's dear life. Joan and I went first to His Majesty's aid. Removing his ill-fitting shoes, we saw that his stockings were not only wet but encrusted with mud and congealing blood. He was icy cold to the touch again, but this time he was not shivering. I was very much afeared he might have caught his death of cold. He was barely conscious, and his voice was slurred with fatigue as he mumbled, "Sweet Mistress Sarah! I thought not to see you here at Boscobel. How I have longed for your tender care and compassion." I could not bring myself to tell him the reason for my presence at Boscobel House, so I simply squeezed his hand and murmured, "Here I am, to care for Your Majesty. Let us make you warm and dry." Joan's kindly eyes were filled with tears to see His Majesty in such a parlous state. "William, we must get these wet clothes off Richard and His Majesty!" she urged. "Sarah has fetched clean night shirts and blankets from the press. Hasten to help these gentlemen out of their wet clothes and into these warm dry things!" Joan and I withdrew to afford the men some privacy, but not before I had time to whisper urgently to William not to remove His Majesty's stockings until we had warm water to hand. I was so troubled that his stockings might be stuck to his blisters and wounds and would pull off more skin if they were removed without soaking.

Once the travellers were modestly clothed again and warmly wrapped in blankets, we womenfolk were allowed back into the parlour to attend to their poorly feet and administer possets. Joan bathed Richard's feet which, thanks to him wearing his own boots, were not badly blistered but very cold and wet. His Majesty explained that the workmen's shoes in which he had been disguised had rubbed and dug into his soft feet which were not used to tramping for miles across rough country. "Then, Your Majesty, I pray you dip your stockinged feet into the basin of water so that I may ease off the stockings without causing you further suffering," I requested. This I was able to do swiftly. His poor feet were piteously blistered and cut, oozing with fresh blood and fluid. I added the sea salt, rosemary and a little honey to the water and tenderly washed His Majesty's feet, much gratified to hear him again sigh with relief as he had done two nights ago when I performed this office for him at White Ladies. I dried his feet with the utmost care and applied softened beeswax and more honey as an ointment, before dressing them in bandages. His Majesty's stockings were much too wet and mired to be put back on. William, seeing this, kindly fetched two pairs of his own, one for His Majesty and one for Richard.

We did not return to our beds that night, but each found a place to sit or lie in the parlour, keeping watchful eyes on His Majesty. Dear Joan brought posset after posset to him and Richard, to warm them inside, to ward off infection and lull them into dozing, albeit fitfully, after so very long without rest. I sat on a tuffet next to His Majesty's chair, with Alice nestled against me, her brown eyes wide with concern for him as I monitored his bodily warmth by periodically placing my hand on his forehead.

As dawn broke, we bestirred ourselves to plan our campaign for the day. It was only to be expected that Parliamentarian soldiers would come to search Boscobel House today since they had been unsuccessful at White Ladies. Joan insisted that we must all have breakfast to line our stomachs for whatever we must face, and cooked a cauldron full of porridge over the fire which we ate with honey and cream. Major Carlis proposed that he and His Majesty should climb one of the great oaks in the woodland behind the house to conceal themselves from Cromwell's men. The remainder of us should engage ourselves in outdoor work as much as possible to look out for soldiers. I wished with all my heart that I could keep His Majesty safe and warm at the fireside. His strength was indeed all spent, and he urgently needed to sleep. Should he get wet again today his life would be in even graver danger from a feverish chill than from the New Model Army.

After we had breakfasted William took a ladder out to the wood to assist Major Carlis and His Majesty in ascending the oak tree. His Majesty's feet were still much afflicted, and he had difficulty walking and climbing in the shoes which had already hurt him so much, but we had none other to give him.

Joan went to the farmyard to feed the chickens and pigs. Alice and I washed up the pots and went about bedmaking which also served as a fine chance to spy out of the upper windows for any signs of the Parliamentarians. After that, we set to breadmaking, skimming cream off the new day's milk from the house cow and churning butter, all of which we would need much in order to sustain the additional souls under this roof. As a guest in William and Joan's home I must repay their hospitality by taking my full share of domestic duties, especially in the straits in which we all found ourselves this day.

The rhythm of household chores gave both Alice and me some peace and calm after the hubbub of the early morning. She asked me, "Mistress Sarah, what will happen to our William if the soldiers catch him?" The thought of that was too awful to contemplate but I had to do my best to reassure the little maid. I swallowed my own emotions and said, "Aah, Alice…. while he is with us, we shall do all we can to make sure that doesn't happen, and Masters Penderel will do their very best to see him to another safe house." But just then Mistress Joan rushed into the kitchen, breathless with news that soldiers were in the woods behind the house.

Boscobel Oak: Saturday 6th
September 1651: Charles

It was so wonderful to be taken into the warmth and comfort of Boscobel House, to be cared for so lovingly and allow myself to rest after those long, painful hours tramping through the dark countryside. Finally, I was able to fall asleep for a while, and Richard too was at last able to let his guard down and doze, safe in the knowledge that William and Major Carlis remained vigilant.

As dawn broke, Mistress Joan made us all breakfast, and too soon Carlis was advising me we must walk out to the woods where we would climb a tree to hide from Cromwell's troops. He selected a fine, tall oak with much foliage, and he and William helped me to walk out to it and climb the ladder William had brought. William watched from the ground to ensure we were quite hidden before taking the ladder back to the house.

The oak's branches were very broad and sturdy, so we were able to perch quite securely. All was quiet at first, and Carlis told me some details of the last throes of the Battle of Worcester, though sadly he had no news of some of my lords who had not been with me to ride away through Saint Martin's Gate that night. Of those who had, all he could tell me was that he believed they had re-joined with Colonel Leslie's Scottish army at Tong Castle, and that Lord Wilmot had repaired to Moseley Hall. I was reassured to know that Henry Wilmot was close by and had my horse safe with his. My lords' rendezvous with the Scots made me sure I had been right not to ride on with them. If the Scots would not obey my command in battle, I could not have been assured, of their protection on the road.

From our lofty hideaway we could see Mistress Joan in the farmyard, and William about his work in the fields. Richard had returned to his own farm, but we knew that his brothers John and George were close at hand guarding nearby lanes under the guise of hedging and ditching. I briefly spied Alice and Mistress Sarah keeping a lookout from the attic windows. But my head was foggy and my eyelids heavy for lack of sleep. Good Carlis saw this and understood. He shifted his position in the tree so that I could rest my head in his lap, and it was not long before I was fast asleep.

My slumber was broken by the sound of voices, and as I woke, Carlis put his hand over my mouth and urgently whispered, "Soldiers!" My stomach lurched and a shiver went down my spine. Peering down through the greenery, we could see Parliamentarian soldiers combing the woods and fields. A small group of them apprehended William and interrogated him. We saw him shaking his head and shrugging his shoulders as if to say he knew nothing about any fugitives.

Those soldiers marched towards the house, but then seemed to decide everything appeared too normal there for it to be harbouring any Cavaliers. Mistress Joan was still in the farmyard, and the kitchen door was open. I could just see Alice's arm turning the butter churn. Mistress Sarah had opened the bedchamber and attic windows too. Among themselves, the womenfolk had contrived a scene of domestic routine which belied the circumstance of a king and a Cavalier soldier hidden just outside the garden.

The day wore on, with periodic sightings of Roundhead soldiers in and around the woods. But William carefully timed an errand to bring us a basket containing a flagon of small beer, some bread and cheese, which we hoisted into the tree on a rope he had flung up to us. Mistress Joan had also sent out a cushion for us. I saw Dame Sarah leading a donkey in the direction of White Ladies and hoped heartily that she would not be apprehended by Parliamentarian soldiers. After that, I must have slept again, my head on the cushion in Carlis' lap, until he apologetically shook me awake because his body had grown so stiff and numb from holding me.

He told me that he had not seen any soldiers for about an hour, and as the sun was now sinking low in the sky, we both hoped that would be the last we would see of them for today. Before long, William came out to the woods with his ladder and signalled to us that he deemed it safe for us to come down and return to the house. Aside from the relief that the threat of capture seemed to have dissipated for the day, Carlis and I were both very glad to stretch our aching limbs and backs from having perched in the oak all day.

White Ladies Manor: Saturday Afternoon 6th September 1651: Sarah

After the fright we had about Cromwell's men in the woods, we were all too much ajangle with nerves to sit down to lunch. William and his brothers, and brother-in-law Francis Yates, had kept discreet watch while going about their agricultural labours. William came into the kitchen to tell us that he had been questioned by the soldiers who had decided Boscobel House was not worthy of raiding since nobody seemed to be guarding it. "They have not discovered His Majesty and Major Carlis, who are well hidden in the oak that has a dense cover of foliage, being pollarded three years back and I can hear no sound from them," he reassured us.

Just as on Thursday morning I felt restive and fretful, but decided it was best to use the afternoon as industriously as possible. I saddled Dorothy's donkey with paniers again and walked him with me back to White Ladies to make amends as best I could in the stillroom. First of all, though, I made a short detour to find the basket I had been forced to abandon. By God's grace it was still where I had left it and had not been disturbed. I turned the donkey loose in his little paddock and took the basket with me to the house.

There was an eerie silence as I walked through the front door. The house felt sad and violated. I could not face my stillroom at first so went into the kitchen to unload the basket and wash up the pots hidden underneath the fruit. Several basins and pancheons lay broken on the floor and I set to clearing up the damage. Suddenly I heard footsteps in the yard and froze with fear, thinking it was the soldiers coming back. Two figures entered through the scullery door and with great relief I saw it was John Penderel and his brother Humphrey the miller. Their capable hands were full of tools and new timber with which to begin repairing the damage wrought by the raiding party. I told them I was most glad to see them, and John answered, "Aye Mistress, and we you. I think we had each other affright. I'm right sorry for the damage done to your stillroom." "Oh John, I haven't been able to go and look yet awhile," I remarked. "Let me put these elderberries to macerate in sugar and I will go to see for myself."

John waited and came up the stairs with me while Humphrey went to begin work in the parlour. The damage was even worse than I had feared. Broken glass mingled with spilled herbs, and overturned bottles, flasks and jars dripped their medicinal tinctures and decoctions from the shelves where they been upset. "Oh John," I exclaimed again, "I don't know where to start!" I was too shocked and saddened to weep. He stood quietly beside me, his broad shoulders hunched in sympathy.

"All your precious work that you do for us all on the Giffard family's estate, Mistress. I am sorry indeed for this ransacking."

His kind words sparked a glimmer of defiance in me. I would not let the soldiers' wickedness stop me from my vocation. "I must clear up and start to replace these mixtures, John, to see us through the winter. We will not let the Parliamentarians have the upper hand over us," I declared as I bent to begin picking up the broken glass. Humphrey kindly brought me one of the largest intact pancheons from the kitchen into which to deposit all the detritus.

It took me many trips to the kitchen midden to clear everything away but at last it was done. It was at least some comfort that nothing would be wasted. The herbs would rot down to feed the soil, and I separated the glass as much as possible so I could use it later as drainage crocks in plant pots, and to deter slugs from my tender seedlings. Some containers had miraculously escaped breakage, and although I would have much work to do to replace those which had been destroyed, I was able to make an inventory of what was missing and most needful of replacement. There were still some herbs flourishing in the garden, although not enough to replenish everything that was lost. At least as it was early autumn I had a goodly chance of foraging rosehips, sloes, blackberries and hazelnuts from the hedgerows in the next few days, and my precious elderberries were safely stowed in the kitchen.

It was growing dark as I walked back to Boscobel, the donkey plodding beside me laden with a sack of Humphrey's newly milled flour lain across his back. I unloaded that at the scullery door and untacked the donkey before turning him out in the orchard. As I walked back towards the house, I spied three figures approaching from the woods. William had been with his ladder to rescue His Majesty and Major Carlis from their hiding place. I noticed how gracefully His Majesty carried himself even though he was so footsore and had been crouched in a tree all day. I hoped fervently that he would not be betrayed by his own regal bearing.

I nipped smartly into the kitchen ahead of them to brew a soothing hyssop tisane to comfort their sore muscles and joints.

Saturday Evening at Boscobel:
6th September 1651: Sarah

T hat evening was as merry a meeting as any of us had enjoyed for many months. Mistress Joan had roasted a chicken and Alice had gathered a basketful of vegetables from the kitchen garden which she had prepared with Joan's guidance in the kitchen while I was at White Ladies. The King's nose twitched most appreciatively as he arrived in the parlour. "Why, Dame Joan," he exclaimed, "you are a marvel to feed two hungry and distressed Cavaliers in such a royal fashion. Roast chicken with thyme and sage, potatoes, kale and broad beans. A feast fit for a King!" We all laughed at his jest.

Major Carlis asked His Majesty to lead us in saying Grace for the feast from the garden and farm. Then William carved the meat and we all sat down to eat together. He provided His Majesty and Major Carlis with a bottle of sack while the rest of us drank small beer. His Majesty called Alice to sit next to him and asked if she had taken a part in preparing the supper. "Yes, Sire…. William," she whispered, "I gathered the vegetables from the garden here and helped Mistress

Joan to cook them." I was astonished, since Alice is usually too shy to speak to anyone other than Dorothy or myself. But the King, for all the difficulties and dangers confronting him, has a natural way of putting people at their ease. "You have done very well, sweet maid," he murmured to her, "this is a most delicious supper." Alice beamed. Emboldened by his compliment, she whispered again to the King, "and there is baked apples and cream for pudding." He licked his lips and pronounced baked apples and cream his favourite dessert. After we had all eaten our fill, William stood to propose a toast to His Majesty to which we all responded in a most heartfelt manner.

William asked His Majesty if there were anything else he desired, upon which our King replied that he would like very much to have a shave. He had three days' uncomfortable growth of beard from being in hiding, and he was minded to add to his disguise by shaving off his Cavalier mustachios. In haste to escape from Worcester, His Majesty's Gentlemen of the Bedchamber had ridden away from White Ladies with his toilette, so William went to fetch his own razor. He lathered His Majesty's face with soap and made to begin shaving him, but his hand shook so much at the thought of performing this service for the King that he declared himself unable to continue. His Majesty asked Major Carlis, but he replied, "I would gladly, Sire, on any other day. But this evening my head is so full of sleep and befuddled by wine that I cannot see straight. I would be afeared of nicking Your Majesty's skin." His Majesty sighed, "Ah well, it seems I must perform this task for myself. But it would have been gratifying to have someone do it for me this evening."

William shot me a meaningful look, suggesting I should volunteer. I spoke up hesitantly, "By your leave, Your Majesty, when I cared for my sick father, I helped him to shave. If Your Majesty is willing to allow me, I will gladly perform this service for you." His face lit up. "Well now, sweet Sarah, this sounds a most pleasant offer and one I will happily accept." So I sat on the couch while His Majesty laid his head on a cushion in my lap. He closed his eyes trustingly and restfully as I carefully scraped away the lather and stubble, and I felt the weight of his head change in my lap as he relaxed. Before I touched his mustachios with the razor I asked him, "Are you quite sure you wish me to shave these off, Sire?" He replied decisively, "Yes, shave 'em off! Without them I have more chance of keeping my head, and they'll grow back quickly enough if I do." His grim humour brought a lump to my throat.

How I wished I had my marigold skin lotion with me to soothe his neck and face afterwards. Joan brought a napkin which she had wrung out in warm water and a few drops of witch hazel decoction; and Alice, who had not strayed from His Majesty's side all evening gently dabbed his face with it, murmuring, "There, there, Sire," while he lapped up her attention, making appreciative sounds and pointing to parts of his face where he wanted more. It was so affecting to see this sweet connexion between them.

Just when I thought we were quite finished, William cleared his throat and said, "Mistress Sarah, if His Majesty is willing, I think he should have his hair trimmed shorter on top in the fashion of countrymen." I was saddened by this, but His Majesty agreed and so, reluctantly I fetched my scissors and comb from my bedchamber. Once again, I wrapped His Majesty's shoulders in my night shawl and began to snip away at his hair under William's instructions. "As short on top as the scissors will do it," he told me, which caused me to weep, my tears falling on His Majesty's poor, cropped head as I worked.

His Majesty forbore this in very good humour and remarked, "Are you washing my hair with your tears, sweet Sarah? This puts me in mind of how Mary of Bethany washed Our Lord's feet with her tears and wiped them away with her hair." "Sire," I replied, "it pains me so much to cut off your beautiful hair, but I do this as a divine office, praying that our heavenly King will keep Your Majesty safe." His hand reached up to mine and brought it to his lips, kissing it tenderly. At last William declared the King's haircut to be in keeping with that of a man of his assumed estate, and I was able to gather up the fallen locks and withdraw to leave the men to drink more sack with Richard who had arrived to discuss with them what was needful for the morrow.

In the kitchen I threw the hair onto the fire and began to wash up the supper pots. Joan and Alice were upstairs in the attic making up a bed on a straw pallet for His Majesty to sleep on in the priest hole. At five feet square it would be a very cramped space for such a tall man to lie in and I worried for his repose. It was several nights since he had known the comfort of a proper bed and his limbs must ache so from walking so far last night and being up in the oak tree all day. Celibate though I am, I longed to take His Majesty into my bed so he could rest his head on a pillow and stretch his long legs, and I could wrap him in my warm arms and watch over him all night while he slept.

Just then Joan came into the kitchen and asked, "Is there still hot water in the cauldron? His Majesty is going to need a warming pan slipped between those sheets before he goes to bed if he is to have any chance of a wink of sleep!" Sweet Joan, to have thought of that. A warming pan would keep him from the cold and assuage his bodily pains.

50

Sunday Rest at Boscobel: 7th September 1651: Charles

It would not quite be truth to say I awoke early on Sunday morning, for I had slept very little all night. Mistress Joan had made the pallet bed as comfortable as she could for me, with her best sheets and a quilt. Kind soul that she is, she had even thought to warm the bed with a warming pan before I retired for the night. Carlis, William and Richard took turns to keep watch overnight. But the priest hole was a very tight hiding place with no room to stretch out my legs, and once its cover was in place it was dark and stuffy. I would much rather have slept in the attic, prepared to dive into the priest hole at a moment's notice if necessary but Richard was insistent that I must be hidden. At my knocking on the cover as the first chinks of daylight flickered between the floorboards, he came to let me out and ask if there were anything I needed immediately. I longed to be outside, gulping in fresh morning air after my night of confinement. Richard thought this too dangerous, so I had to content myself with walking about in the attic which at least allowed my legs to ease their stiffness. I said my prayers and recited the holy office of Matins from memory.

After a while Richard returned to the attic to tell me it was safe for the time being to come downstairs and have some breakfast. The fresh bread and butter tasted very good, and Mistress Joan brought me some honey and a cup of small beer. There was no sign of William or Carlis, whom Richard told me had gone to a neighbouring farm to procure a sheep for a dinner of mutton to be eaten later in the day. Mistress Joan nipped between the kitchen and the parlour, fussing maternally over me to ensure I had everything I desired and that I was warm enough. "How did Your Majesty sleep?" she asked. "I was so fretful for you trussed up in that priest hole with your long legs. I hardly nodded off all night myself for worrying about you!" I told her how grateful I was for her thoughtfulness and that I had been quite comfortable, but I doubt she believed me, seeing my haggard face and stiff limbs.

When William and Carlis arrived back at the house with the meat, they fell into discussion with Richard and myself about whether I should be allowed outside. Richard was still very wary of this, but William and Carlis reported having seen no Parliamentarian soldiers on their errand and they reminded Richard that the soldiers had been convinced yesterday that Boscobel was not worthy of a search party. For myself, I doubted that the Puritans would come looking even for a fugitive king on the Lord's Day. So Richard agreed cautiously that I take could a little turn around the garden which I very gladly did.

The day was dry and pleasant, and it felt good to be outside in daylight after so many hours spent travelling at night and cooped up in confined spaces. My feet were still very sore so I was not able to walk much, but sat a while to appreciate the garden and the Shropshire countryside beyond. Presently, Mistress Sarah and Alice came by on their way back from feeding the animals in the farmyard. Alice was carrying a basket of eggs and Sarah had a pail of milk. Although this way of life seemed strange to me, I could not but admire and feel even a little envious of the close harmony in which this household lived with Nature to provide for their needs.

We greeted each other and Mistress Sarah enquired, "Sire, how are you this morning? Are your feet still troubling you sorely? And how did you sleep?" As with Mistress Joan, I tried to pass off my night in the priest hole as more comfortable than it had really been, but Dame Sarah is very shrewd and replied that a nap by the fireside might be a good remedy. "And by your leave, Your Majesty, I will tend to your feet again shortly." I assented and watched her and Alice go on their way into the kitchen.

A moment later, William came out to dig. I watched in fascination as he unearthed potatoes and carrots for our midday meal. Not long afterwards, Sarah came back with her basket, cutting leaves from the vegetable plot and herb garden. I called to her to ask what she was harvesting, and she came to me, smiling as she held out a sprig for me to smell, whereupon I recognised the aroma of mint. Then off she went again to the pond just outside the garden, cutting sappy twigs and leaves from a willow growing there.

I began to feel hungry and repaired to the parlour, wondering when lunch might be ready. Sounds and scents of food preparation came from the kitchen, and presently Carlis appeared from the cellar with a haunch of mutton. Mindful that everyone in the household except me had taken their part in making the meal ready, I asked Mistress Joan if I might have a frying pan and some butter to fry some collops of mutton on the fire. She obliged, although she looked a little askance at me as if wondering what sort of showing I should make of cooking the meat. I cut several pieces of meat from the joint and started to fry them. It felt elemental to work at the fire and made me feel a little more aligned to the household's connexion with the earth and the animals, which I had witnessed in the garden.

Mistress Joan and Alice brought platters and dishes to the table, and soon we were all gathered for the meal. "Why, Sire, you have done very well with the mutton!" declared Mistress Joan. It was gratifying to think I had done so while in receipt of such hospitality and kindness from these dear people who had not hesitated to shelter and care for me, despite risking their own lives to do so. I winked at Mistress Joan and declared myself to the master cook of Boscobel House. She wagged her finger playfully back at me.

After the meal, Mistress Sarah asked to bathe my feet again. She had prepared a poultice of the willow I had seen her gathering earlier and applied this warm to my wounds. I found this very soothing, and she recommended, if I could bear it, to keep my feet bare for a while to let the skin breathe without the constriction of those shoes. She and Carlis helped me outside to a little arbour in the garden where I passed a very pleasant afternoon reading in the early autumn sunshine. Sarah kept me company for some of the time, working at her embroidery before dressing my feet with more honey and beeswax, and binding them with clean linen bandages.

At about six of the clock Richard and his brothers arrived to consult with William and myself about my removal to Moseley Hall which John had secured in a meeting with Father Huddleston, a recusant priest sheltered by the master of the house, Mr Whitgreave who is a Catholic gentleman very faithful to the Crown. The arrangements were marred for me only by the news that Harry Wilmot, with whom I looked forward to being reunited, had left Moseley Hall and repaired to Bentley Hall some miles farther on.

56

Departure for Moseley Hall:
Sunday 7th September 1651: Sarah

When His Majesty was ready to leave for Moseley, we all gathered in the hall to say our farewells. He drew each of us aside in turn to speak a few private words.

When my turn came, he placed his hand around my waist and took me back into the parlour to say, "Sweetest Sarah, how can I ever thank you enough for all your loving care of me these past few days? Without your ministrations I think I would have died of cold or exhaustion." "Nay Sire," I demurred. "I have done very little. Mistress Joan and the Penderel brothers have done so much more to save your precious life." "Each of you have taken an important part, I own," he acknowledged, "but you have shown me the tenderest compassion and have used your healing knowledge of herbs to cure my ills. And although it grieved you so deeply to do it, I might not have survived thus far had you not cut my hair. I shall never forget your loving service, and if I live to come into my Kingdom in England I pray that you will visit me at Court." I made my curtsey, bowing my head to hide the tears that once more fell from my eyes, and tried to protest that Richard and his brothers had guarded him so well that nobody except his loyal subjects had seen him. His Majesty kissed his own finger and placed it to my lips, silencing me.

Then he took both my hands in his to raise me, and cupped my face in his hands, gently kissing away my tears. "Farewell, sweetest Sarah," he whispered before kissing me on the lips. "Farewell, and God speed you safely to France, my liege lord; and may He bring you into your kingdom," I responded. "You know, I hope, that you are already King in the hearts of all who have served you here, and many more in England."

And then he was gone, swept out into the evening chill by Richard who was waiting with his brothers and Francis to accompany His Majesty to Moseley Hall. Humphrey had brought his aged mill horse for His Majesty to ride since his feet were still very sore and swollen. The distance from Boscobel to Moseley is five miles, but the brothers planned to take His Majesty by winding lanes away from the highway to evade detection.

We all stepped out of the house to wave off the little party and wish His Majesty "Godspeed," again. Alice and I waved until the horse disappeared into the dark evening and the lanterns George and John carried could no longer be seen. On the breeze, I thought I heard His Majesty complain that Humphrey's horse was "the dullest, heaviest jade I have ever ridden," and then Humphrey's strong voice more clearly, retorting jovially, "Sire, no wonder the horse is slow. He is carrying the weight of three kingdoms upon his back." And so, I handed on His Majesty to others whom I prayed would love and care for him as much as our household had done, on his perilous journey into exile. Although I must let him go, I knew that I would treasure in my heart the events of these past few days for the rest of my life, when our King gave himself so trustfully into my care.

Epilogue: Christmas Eve at White Ladies Manor 1651: Sarah

It was Christmas Eve and at White Ladies, as in other households up and down the land, we were preparing for another Christmas under harsh Puritanical rule. Although we were allowed to mark the Nativity of Our Lord by attendance at a plain church service on the Sunday nearest to Christmas Day, we were to sing no hymns or carols, nor to venerate His blessed mother Our Lady Saint Mary. Neither must we decorate our home with holly, ivy and mistletoe as had previously been the custom. There were to be no presents exchanged; and eating and drinking were to be no more than sufficient for an ordinary day. Instead of the customary seasonal merriment, mirth and misrule, Christmas was to be marked by contemplation of our sins in holy solemnity. We would have very much liked to hear the Holy Mass said in the secret chapel at Boscobel House on Christmas Day, but it was too dangerous for Father Huddleston to travel from Moseley Hall to outlying houses with his missal and the sacraments.

I was in my herb garden cutting a few sage leaves from a bush I had placed in a sheltered position by an old wall, to make a stuffing for the joint of pork we would share as a household on the holy day, when a rider of military bearing came to the gate. My heart seemed to stop in my chest. Surely the Puritans would not send a soldier to so isolated a place to spy on our preparations for Christmas! Could they be set to punish us because we had sheltered His Majesty?

But the horseman saluted me and introduced himself as Colonel Lane from Bentley Hall. "Good morrow, Colonel Lane," I greeted him. "How welcome you are. Will you come into the house for some refreshment?" He graciously accepted, first leading his big chestnut horse into the stable and providing him with hay and water. Dorothy made the Colonel very welcome in the parlour, furnishing him with mulled cider and sweetmeats.

Alice peeped cautiously through the drawing room doorway, and Colonel Lane beckoned her to come to him. "Miss Alice, my sister Jane has told me about your kindness to His Majesty, and she would like you to have this in recognition of your faithful service to him." He drew from his pocket a beautifully worked hussif stocked with sewing needles, pearl topped pins, a silver thimble and scissors wrought in the same design. Alice was quite overcome, but her face lit up with delight. I drew her to me and exclaimed with her at the loveliness of each object until she summoned the courage to bob a curtsey and thank him for the gift.

After some time in pleasant conversation, the Colonel begged leave to speak with me privately. He told me how the King was cared for by many people after leaving Boscobel House: firstly by Mr Whitgreave and Father Huddleston at Moseley Hall, who continued to tend his poor feet and gave him a shirt of fine flax to wear in place of the unbleached rough linen one which had chafed his skin so. From there he went on to Bentley Hall from whence the Colonel's own sister, Mistress Jane Lane bravely rode pillion, with His Majesty disguised as her servant, to Bristol, even right through a troop of Parliamentarian soldiers in the village of Wootton Wawen near Stratford upon Avon.

I learned of the numerous households which sheltered and nourished His Majesty throughout the West Country, and how his trusted friend Lord Wilmot rode before him to broker such arrangements. It was a wonder he were not apprehended, since unlike His Majesty, the noble lord had resolutely refused to be disguised, save for carrying a hawk on his wrist and having spaniels at his horse's heels, as if he were out hunting.

Colonel Lane further advised me of His Majesty's jeopardy as ships he had hoped to board at Bristol, Lyme Regis and Bridport all failed. His Majesty undertook further identities as an eloping bridegroom with Mistress Juliana Coningsby, and as a merchant escaping a duel over debts.

Eventually after six weeks as a hunted man, he was safely delivered onto a coal brig called The Surprise at Shoreham in Sussex which carried him safely to Fécamp in France from whence he travelled to Rouen and thence to Paris, where he was reunited with his mother Queen Henrietta Maria and his brother Prince James, Duke of York at The Louvre Palace. This gave me especial delight, as I remembered that during his time with us at White Ladies and Boscobel I had been acutely aware of how young His Majesty was, and how much in need of a mother's love and care he seemed in the terrible circumstances of his defeat at Worcester and the threat to his life. What a joyous celebration of Christmas it would be for our King and his mother now that they could be together again, far away from those who sought to take his life.

The Colonel reassured me that Lord Wilmot and Major Carlis had both safely joined His Majesty in Paris, as indeed had Mistress Lane, who escaped from Bentley Hall even as Parliamentarian soldiers were on their way there to arrest her for high treason. She walked across England, almost two hundred miles, disguised as a beggar, to King's Lynn where she caught a cargo ship to Rouen.

"Mistress Sarah," he continued, "I have here a letter for you which has been passed hand to hand from the Royal Court at Fontainebleau where His Majesty presently resides under the protection of his cousin, His Majesty King Louis XIV of France." Colonel Lane handed me a letter sealed plainly with no signet and bade me open it. Inside, I found an exquisite gold brooch set with a sapphire which signifies healing, chastity and fulfilment, and a curl of black hair tied with a ribbon of the same shade of blue as His Majesty's Garter riband, just enough to conceal in the locket chamber at the back of the brooch. The letter itself was very brief, simply a few words which were, "To sweetest Sarah from CR with love and deepest gratitude." A secret Christmas gift from my sovereign Charles Rex, which meant more to me than any words could ever tell.

Bibliography

Ainsworth, William Harrison (1874) *Boscobel, or The Royal Oak: A tale of the year 1651:* Routledge (Kindle version)

Culpeper, N (first published 1653) *The Complete Herbal* 2019 edition Steven Foster (ed): Sterling

Culpeper, N (first published 1652) *The English Physician* 2016 edition: Wentworth Press

Fox, S and Brazier, M (2020) 'The regulation of midwives in England, c1500-1902' *Medical Law International Volume 20, issue 4,* pages 308-338 *The regulation of midwives in England, c.1500–1902 - Sarah Fox, Margaret Brazier, 2020 (sagepub.com)*

Fraser, A (2002) *King Charles II:* Weidenfeld and Nicolson

Gerard, J (first published 1597) *Herbal* 2015 edition: Noverre Press

Gregory, P (2019) *Tidelands:* Simon and Schuster

Heyer, Georgette (2005) *Royal Escape:* Arrow (first published in 1938 by William Heinemann)

Hughes, J (2017) *The Boscobel Tracts, Relating to the Escape of Charles the Second After the Battle of Worcester and His*

Subsequent Adventures: HardPress (Kindle version)

The above contains Boscobel, or The History of His Sacred Majesty's Miraculous Preservation after the Battle of Worcester parts i and ii by Thomas Blount (1660) and The King's Narrative edited by Samuel Pepys (1680)

Maxwell-Hudson, Clare (1995) *Aromatherapy Massage*: Dorling-Kindersley

Minkowski, W (1992) 'Women healers of the middle ages: selected aspects of their history' *American Journal of Public Health* Volume 82 Number 2 Published online 2011 *Women healers of the middle ages: selected aspects of their history. | AJPH | Vol. 82 Issue 2 (aphapublications.org)*

Spencer, Charles (2017) *To Catch a King*: William Collins

Wilson, L (2016) *The History Girls: Woman healers of the Seventeenth Century, by Leslie Wilson (the-history-girls.blogspot. com)*

Wynn, R (2000) *Saints and Sinners: Women and the Practice of Medicine Throughout the Ages | JAMA | JAMA Network* Journal of the American Medical Association Volume 283, Number 5, pages 668-669

English Heritage information online

English Heritage History of White Ladies Priory

Boscobel House and the Royal Oak History Charles II and the Royal Oak

National Trust information online

Moseley Old Hall | National Trust

Glossary

Billhook: A heavy duty tool with a short handle and a long blade for cutting woody material such as thin branches or coppice poles

Biscuit: Alternatively called hardtack, this is a cracker-like food made from flour, water and salt. It was used on military campaigns and was useful in domestic homes as a non-perishable basic foodstuff

Collops: Slices, or possibly small chunks, of meat

Coppice: A small wood of trees, often of hazel or willow. Coppicing is the practice of cutting the stems of such trees to the ground every few years, for making fencing, hurdles to enclose livestock, or plant supports such as bean poles.

Copse: Another name for a small wood of trees, although these may be of a wider variety than in a coppice

Dame: A courtesy title for an older woman, often used interchangeably with Mistress for a lay woman. It is also a title which would have been used for a nun.

Decoction: Concentrated liquor made by boiling a plant substance such as leaves, flowers or roots. Usually made for medicinal purposes

Fealty: Loyalty expressed to a monarch or aristocrat

Garter riband: A broad ribbon or sash worn with the Order of the Garter insignia

Hussif: Also known as a Housewife, this is a box or fabric container for needlework tools, a sewing kit

Infirmarian: A senior monk or nun who is skilled in herbal medicine, healing and care of sick and dying people.

Liege: A title used to address an aristocrat or monarch with whom one is in direct allegiance

Macerate: To allow fruit and sugar to mix naturally together over several hours so that the fruit's juices are released

Midden: A domestic rubbish heap which would include household and human waste. A kitchen midden might have been separate from that of human waste, although both would have been used to fertilise the garden

Missal: Roman Catholic book of prayers, responses and orders of service for Mass

Pancheon: A large earthenware basin or bowl for making bread

Pillion: A saddle with extra seating for another rider behind the one controlling the horse

Pollard: A tree which has had the top growth off a tree to encourage it to produce new branches and foliage. Pollarding is the practice of cutting trees in this way

Posset: A heated mixture of milk or cream with wine added to it, used to ward off or drive out infections

Recusant: A person refusing to comply with a regulation or authority. Roman Catholics were known as recusants under Puritan rule in England because they refused to convert to Protestantism, even though Roman Catholicism was officially outlawed

Sack: A type of dry, fortified white wine similar to, but not the same as, sherry. It is likely to have been the alcoholic ingredient in the possets prepared for His Majesty and Richard Penderel

Small beer: A very weak type of beer which was commonly drunk by adults and children because water was not considered safe to drink

Stillroom: A room or space for drying or otherwise processing herbs for domestic or medicinal purposes.

Tincture: Medicinal remedy made by dissolving a drug or herb in alcohol

Tisane: Herbal tea made either with fresh or dried plant material or by diluting a decoction in hot water

Toilette: A case containing personal washing and grooming products and tools

Questions and Discussion Points for Book Clubs and Reading Groups

Before reading this book, how much did you know about Charles' escape from the Battle of Worcester?

What, if anything, have you learned from reading this book?

Which chapter of the book resonates most strongly with you, and can you say why?

Which character (real or fictional) do you most relate to in the book, and can you say why?

How did you feel when reading the book, and what feelings have stayed with you, if any?

Would reading this story make you wish to find out more about the six weeks in which Charles was a fugitive?

How well do you think the device of blending historical fact with fiction works in this book?

How well do you feel the telling of the story from both Sarah's and Charles' perspective works?

What is your reaction to the religious references in the book?

How do you respond to the book's narrative about herbalism?

Is there anything that you feel the book is lacking?

Do you feel the author has achieved her goal of writing the account in a feminine register?

The author explains in her preface how vividly she was affected by her visit to Boscobel House, which led to writing this book. Have you had any similar experiences, and can you share these?

Is Sarah a feminist? Discuss.

If you were going to make a film of the book, who would you cast as Charles? And Sarah? Are there other characters for whom you can imagine casting a particular actor? Who, and why?

What messages can we take away from reading this book which apply to modern life? Perhaps in supporting refugees or other people forced to turn to strangers for support, shelter and nourishment?

Does the book remind you of other novels you have read? If so, which ones, and in what ways?

Should the story of Charles' escape should be in the History curriculum in schools? What reasons would you give for your answer?

If you were to compile a playlist based on this book, which songs or pieces of music would you include? As a couple of starters, the author included 'Times Like These' by The Foo Fighters and 'Gimme Shelter' by The Rolling Stones in hers.

Acknowledgements

This book would never have come into being had my very dear friend Diane Reardon-Smith not suggested a day out at Boscobel House. It was a life-changing experience! I thank her deeply for that, and for being one of a small number of trusted family, friends and colleagues who have read the manuscript and have given me valuable feedback.

My other lovely friends Lucy Bond, Julia Bristow, Erika Kirk, Liz Lester, Barbara Perry and Terry Turvey are those to whom I am also very grateful for feedback and encouragement to publish.

I give my heartfelt thanks to everyone at UK Book Publishing who have guided and supported me through the publishing process.

I am very grateful to my lovely daughter Catherine Wellington, who has given expert advice about the location of the French royal court in 1651, and on Charles' wider family.

Finally, I thank my wonderful husband Jim Wellington for proof-reading my work so diligently and for putting up so patiently with my sudden obsession with a young and vulnerable King Charles II.

Any remaining mistakes or omissions are my own.

About the Author

Hilary Wellington lives in Nottinghamshire, England with her husband, daughter and larger-than-life cat. She read Sociology and Social History at the University of York and has an MA in Women's Studies and an M.Ed in Inclusive Education. Hilary has had a lifelong fascination with herbs and herbal medicine and has been a keen hand stitcher since her teens. She has enjoyed incorporating both interests in this book.

Hilary is a lifelong learning practitioner in her day job, having taught health and social care, and counselling studies, to adults at the Open University and the University of Leicester. She currently works in community adult education, teaching a variety of courses on mental health, person-centred communication, learning differences and crafting for wellbeing.

A King's Sanctuary is her first book of fiction.